Joyce Dunbar • Petr Horáček

GRUMPY DUCK

Duck was feeling grumpy.
The pond was dry so she
couldn't paddle in it.
She had no one to play with.

A little grey cloud appeared over her head.

THIS WALKER BOOK BELONGS TO

....

For the ARVON FOUNDATION, which
helped to make this book happen – J.D. and P.H.

First published 2018 by Walker Books Ltd, 87 Vauxhall Walk, London SE11 5HJ
This edition published 2019

2 4 6 8 10 9 7 5 3 1

Text © 2018 Joyce Dunbar
Illustrations © 2018 Petr Horáček

This book has been set in Sabon and Warugaki

Printed in China

British Library Cataloguing in Publication Data:
a catalogue record for this book is available from the British Library

ISBN 978-1-4063-8296-9

www.walker.co.uk

WALKER BOOKS
AND SUBSIDIARIES
LONDON • BOSTON • SYDNEY • AUCKLAND

She waddled over to Dog, who was digging a hole.

"I've got no one to play with," she said to Dog.

"You can play with me," said Dog, "if you like digging holes."

"I don't," grumped Duck. "Digging holes would
make my feathers dirty."

"Hu-huh," sighed Dog.

The little grey cloud got **BIGGER**.

Pig was rolling in the mud.

"I've got no one to play with," Duck said to Pig.

"Come and play with me," said Pig, "in my pongy puddle."

"No thanks," grumped Duck. "Ducks like ponds, not pongs."

"Oooonk," honked Pig.

The little grey cloud got even **BIGGER**.

Cockerel was cockadoodling.

"I've got no one to play with," said Duck.

"You can play with me if you like," said Cockerel.

"We could sing a cockadoodle chorus."

"I just don't do cockadoodling,"
grumped Duck.

"Squawk!" went Cockerel.

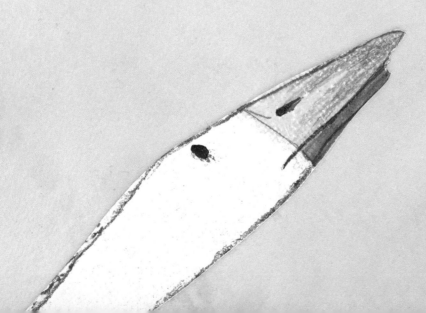

The little grey cloud got **BIGGER** still.

Rabbit was hopping around.

"I've got no one to play with," said Duck.

"Come and hop with me," said Rabbit.

"We can see who can hop the highest."

"*You* can, silly!" grumped Duck.

"I'm *not* silly," said Rabbit.

The little grey cloud
wasn't little
any more –
it was
BIG.

Tortoise was dozing in his shell.

"I've got no one to play with," said Duck,

tapping his shell with her beak.

"You can doze with me," said Tortoise. "It's very peaceful."

"Boring more like," grumped Duck.

"Tut," tutted Tortoise.

Now the grey cloud was

HUGE.

"Cheer up Duck," said Goat, who
was busy eating the washing on the line.
"I've got no one to play with," said Duck.
"Share a snack with me," said Goat.
"Here's a tasty T-shirt."

"Ducks don't eat clothes," grumped Duck.

"And neither do goats. You'll get a stomach ache."

"Oh, will I?" grumbled Goat.

Now the great grey cloud was

GINORMOUS!

It was a great grey blob hanging low overhead,
so now ALL of the animals were grumpy.

Then something strange began to happen.
The great grey cloud turned blue and purple
and yellow until it was

BLACK!

Sitting beneath this ginormous black cloud was ...

a dog who had stopped wagging his tail,

a pig whose ears were droopy,

a cockerel who no longer cockadoodled,

a rabbit who had lost his hop,

a tortoise who had decided to stay in his shell for ever and ever,

a goat who scowled at the big black cloud

and a duck who was **still** grumpy.

What sort of cloud was it?

Was it a GLOOM cloud?

Or a MOOD cloud?

Could it be … was it …

a GRUMPY DUCK cloud?

Would it blot out the sun for ever?

Could it BURST?

YES,

for suddenly there was a

SPLATT **PLOP**

PLINK **DRIBBLE**

PLITTER PLATT

MILLIONS OF BIG SHINY

WET SPLASHY RAINDROPS!

Duck spread her wings wide open.

She splished and splashed and sploshed.

Duck wasn't grumpy any more.

"I'm waddling in the rain.

QUACK! QUACK!"

she sang.

One by one they all joined in.

"I'm plopping in the rain. OINK! OINK!"

"I'm barking in the rain. WOOF! WOOF!"

"I'm COCKADOODLING in the rain!"

"I'm hopping so high. HIP-HOP!"

"I'm drinking up the rain. SLURP! SLURP!"

COCKADOODLE-DO

HIP-HOP

QUACK
QUACK

SLURP SLURP

"What a glorious feeling," bleated Goat.
"We're happy again, just waddling, and paddling,
by the pond," they all sang in chorus.
And where was the big black cloud?

Gone!

In its place

was a bright shining

RAINBOW.

THE END